Florence
the Friendship
Fairy

Special thanks to Sue Mongredien

For Hannah Powell, who gave
me the idea for Florence in
the first place. Thank you!

ORCHARD BOOKS

First published in Great Britain in 2011 by Orchard Books
This edition published in 2016 by The Watts Publishing Group

22

© 2016 Rainbow Magic Limited.
© 2016 HIT Entertainment Limited.
Illustrations © Orchard Books 2011

HIT entertainment

A CIP catalogue record for this book is available from the British Library.

ISBN 978 1 40831 238 4

Printed and bound by CPI Group (UK) Ltd, Croydon, CR0 4YY

MIX
Paper from
responsible sources
FSC® C104740

The paper and board used in this book are made from wood from responsible sources

Orchard Books
An imprint of Hachette Children's Group
Part of The Watts Publishing Group Limited
Carmelite House, 50 Victoria Embankment, London EC4Y 0DZ

An Hachette UK Company
www.hachette.co.uk
www.hachettechildrens.co.uk

Florence

the Friendship Fairy

by Daisy Meadows

ORCHARD

The fairies are planning a Friendship Day
But I'll soon take their smiles away.
I'll spoil it all, I'll wreck their fun
I'll break the friendships one by one.

I'll steal Florence's magic things
And laugh at the misery this brings!
A ribbon, a book, a bracelet too
She really won't know what to do.

Friendship will be finished, wait and see.
Soon everyone will be friendless, just like me!

The Memory Book

Contents

Magic Memories   11

Friendship...and Frost!   19

On the Goblin Trail   27

Boo!   37

A Tempting Offer   47

Magic Memories

Rachel Walker took a large scrapbook from underneath Kirsty Tate's bed, then the two best friends opened it between them. It was their memory book, full of souvenirs from all the fun and exciting times they'd shared together.

"That holiday on Rainspell Island was so special," Rachel said, pointing at the ferry tickets and map which had been stuck in.

"I know," Kirsty smiled. "It was the first time we met each other – and the first time we met the fairies, too!" She lowered her voice. "I wonder if we'll have a fairy adventure this week?"

"I hope so," Rachel said, feeling her heart thump excitedly at the thought. She'd just arrived to spend the half-term holiday with Kirsty's family, and had been wondering the same thing herself. Somehow, extra-special things always seemed to happen when the girls got together!

The friends went on looking through their book. There was the museum leaflet from the day they'd met Storm the Lightning Fairy, tickets to Strawberry Farm where they'd helped Georgia the Guinea Pig Fairy, all sorts of photos, postcards, maps, petals and leaves...

Then Kirsty frowned as she saw an empty space on one page. "Has a picture fallen out?" she wondered.

"It must have," Rachel said. "You can see the marks where something was stuck in before.

I think it was a photo of the fairy models we made the day we met Willow the Wednesday Fairy. I wonder where it's gone?"

As the girls turned the pages, they realised that the photo wasn't the only thing missing. A constellation map Kirsty's gran had given them the night they'd helped Stephanie the Starfish Fairy had vanished, as well as the all-access pass they'd had for the Fairyland Olympics. Then came even worse discoveries.

"Oh no! This photo of us at Camp Stargaze is torn," Rachel said in dismay.

"This page has scribbles on," Kirsty cried. "How did that happen?"

"And where did *this* picture come from?" Rachel asked, pointing at a colourful image of a pretty little fairy. She had shoulder-length blonde hair that was pinned back with a pink, star-shaped hair clip. She wore a sparkly lilac top and a ruffled blue skirt with a colourful belt around her middle, and pink sparkly ankle boots. "I've never even seen her before!" She bit her lip. "Something weird is going on, Kirsty. You don't think..."

Before she could finish her sentence, the picture of the fairy began to sparkle and glitter with all the colours of the rainbow.

The girls watched, wide-eyed, as the fairy fluttered her wings, gave a stretch, and then flew right out from the page in a whirl of twinkling dust!

"Oh!" gasped Kirsty. "Hello! What's your name...and how did you get into our memory book?"

The fairy smiled, shook out her wings

and flew a loop-the-loop.

"I'm Florence the Friendship Fairy," she said in a tinkling voice, her bright eyes darting around the room. "And you're Kirsty and Rachel, aren't you? I've heard so much about you! I know you've been good friends to the fairies many, many times."

"It's lovely to meet you," Rachel said. "But Florence, do you know what's happened to our memory book? Things are missing from it, and some have even been spoiled."

Florence fluttered to land on the bed. "I'm afraid that's the reason I came here," she said sadly. "Special memory books, scrapbooks and photograph albums everywhere have been spoiled, or even stolen – and I need your help!"

Friendship...
and Frost!

The girls were puzzled, so Florence explained. "As the friendship fairy, I do my best to keep friendships strong throughout the human world, and the fairy world, too," she said. "And, like you, I have a memory book which I fill with my nicest friendship memories – party invitations, pressed flowers, pictures..."

"Sounds lovely," Rachel said with
a smile.

"It is," Florence replied. "Best of all, it's
full of special friendship magic. While my
book is with me, its magic protects all the
special mementos of friendship made
and collected by friends all over the
world, and keeps the wonderful memories
inside them safe. But unfortunately..."

"Don't tell me – Jack Frost has done something horrible again!" Kirsty added crossly. Jack Frost was a mean, spiky creature who was always doing spiteful things, helped by his sneaky goblin servants.

"Yes," said Florence glumly. "Jack Frost doesn't believe in friendship," she went on. "I think he's jealous of other people having best friends and doing fun things together – because he doesn't *have* any friends. Everyone is too scared of him."

Rachel and Kirsty nodded. They had met Jack Frost several times, and he was scary. He was always so bad-tempered and fierce – and he had very strong magical powers too, unfortunately.

"We fairies have been planning a special Friendship Day for tomorrow,"

Florence told them. "The Party Fairies have been helping get everything ready – the music, the outfits, the party games, the food... Oh, it's going to be so much fun! But when I was in the party workshop, I put down my memory book for a moment so that I could help Cherry the Cake Fairy with her icing. Before I knew what was happening, the goblins had burst in and stolen my book!"

"Oh, no!" cried Rachel. "That's awful."

"Is that why *our* memory book has been spoiled, too?" Kirsty asked.

"Yes," Florence said. "Since my memory book was taken, other people's books and photograph albums haven't been magically protected. No doubt, the goblins have seized the chance to go around spoiling as many of them as they can!"

"Well, we'll help you find your magic book," Rachel said at once, her eyes gleaming with excitement at the thought of another fairy adventure. "Where do you think we should start looking?"

"Oh, thank you!" Florence said. "True friends always help each other." She fluttered over to perch on Kirsty's knee.

"I've been following the goblins' trail –
they're definitely in the human world,
and they've obviously been here in
Wetherbury, as they've messed up your
book. So we could have a look around
the village – do you think your parents
will let you do that?"

"Yes," Kirsty replied. "Wetherbury is
only small, and I know most people
here, so Mum and Dad are fine about
me being out, as long as I'm with a
friend and I tell them where we're going.

Maybe if we..." She broke off as she heard footsteps approaching. "Quick, Florence! Hide!" she whispered urgently.

On the Goblin Trail

With a whirl of sparkly fairy dust,
Florence fluttered her wings and flew
back into the book, where she became
a picture on the page once more.

Rachel smiled. Fairy magic was *so*
brilliant!

Kirsty's mum came into the room,
holding her purse and a shopping bag.

"Girls, I'm just about to do a baking session for the village hall party and need a couple of things picking up from the shop. I don't suppose you'd mind—"

"We'll get them," Kirsty interrupted at once, flashing a grin at Rachel. "What do you need?"

Kirsty's mum wrote them a list, and opened her purse. The party she'd mentioned was being held in two days' time to celebrate the reopening of the village hall. Everyone in the village had helped to restore the hall to its former glory and was planning to go to the party – it sounded like it was going to be great fun.

While Mrs Tate was looking in her purse, Florence gave Rachel a cheeky wink, then flew out of the memory book in a flurry of pink sparkles, and fluttered to hide in Rachel's pocket. Kirsty's mum looked up just as the last sparkle of magic dust disappeared – phew! – and gave Kirsty some money.

The girls set off, with Florence peeping out of Rachel's pocket. They hadn't gone very far when they spotted a colourful bit of paper blowing about on the ground. Rachel pounced on it immediately.

"Look, Kirsty, it's the ticket to the flower show where we met Ella the Rose Fairy," she said. "The goblins must have dropped it."

"So we know they went this way!" Kirsty said excitedly, putting the paper carefully into her bag. She stared around the lane, hoping to spot a flash of goblin green. "Let's head for the main street."

The girls walked down Twisty Lane and passed the village hall. It was already hung with bunting in preparation for the party, and looked very smart with its fresh paint.

As she was admiring it, Kirsty spotted something that had been dropped in a bush at the entrance to the hall's small car park. "It's a sweet wrapper," she said, picking it up and showing Rachel the shiny red paper. "But not an ordinary one."

"I recognise that!" Florence said eagerly. "Strawberry Sparkles – they're made by Honey the Sweet Fairy!"

Rachel smiled, remembering the adventure they'd had with Honey. It had definitely been one of the tastiest fairy missions they'd been on! "And that wrapper is from our memory book too. We're still on the trail!"

The girls carried on walking and were just passing the park when they heard the sound of harsh, grumpy voices raised in argument. "Stop smiling, you look awful," one voice complained. "And you two, stop pushing each other."

"He keeps jabbing me with that nettle," another voice moaned. "Gerroff!"

"Ouch!"

The girls and Florence looked at each other. "Sounds like goblins!" Florence whispered excitedly. "Let's take a closer look."

Kirsty and Rachel slipped into the
park and hid behind a large flowering
bush. They peeped through the leaves
to see five bickering goblins who were
jostling one another as they posed for
a photograph.

"Ready?" called a sixth goblin. "Say...
UGLY!"

"UGLY!" they chorused, all leering
horribly at the camera.

"Perfect," said the goblin with the camera. "So we've got a photo, some dirt, a nettle, a few weeds... Our memory book is really coming along."

"Our stuff is way better than that silly fairy's," scoffed one of the other goblins. "Flowers and fairy dust and all sorts of pink stuff... Yuck!"

"Come on, let's go and find some more things," the tallest goblin ordered.

"Put what you've collected in your pockets, and don't forget the yucky fairy book. Jack Frost said we weren't allowed to let it out of our sight."

The goblins marched out of the park, heading for the main street. One was carrying a book with a purple and gold cover and Florence stiffened as she saw it.

"There's my book!" she cried. "We've got to get it back. Follow those goblins!"

Boo!

Kirsty and Rachel hung back until
the goblins were a safe distance away,
then began following them along
Twisty Lane. The goblins all seemed in
very good moods, and kept stopping to
take photographs of one another. But
these photos weren't like ones taken for
ordinary memory books or albums –
instead, the goblins got the camera out
for the strangest things.

"Take one of me with this great big snail!" one goblin cried eagerly, picking up a large snail and balancing  it on his head. "Lovely and slimy!"

"Take one of us having a fight," another goblin suggested, as he elbowed a skinny goblin with knobbly knees.

"Hey, get off!" yelled the skinny goblin, lashing out.

Snap! Snap! went the camera at the snail, the fight, and then the pile of litter that another goblin found. "Ahh, this is what good memories are all about," sniggered the smallest goblin who had mean, squinty eyes. "Hey, what about a photo of me ripping up this soppy fairy book? That would be brilliant!"

Florence gasped as he grabbed the memory book and made as if to tear it with his warty green fingers. "No!" she cried, zooming through the air before Kirsty or Rachel could stop her. "Don't do that!"

The goblins swung round at the sound of her silvery voice. "Oh, great," the tallest one moaned. "Just what we *didn't* want. A silly pink fairy come to spoil everything. Quick, lads. Run!"

The goblins sprinted away, with the small, mean goblin still holding Florence's precious memory book. As he ran, pretty flowers and sparkly treasures dropped from its pages, and Florence looked as if she wanted to cry.

"They're ruining it!" she wailed,
swooping down and waving her magic
wand to make
all the items
fairy-size,
and collect
together
everything
that had
fallen out.

Meanwhile, the
goblins were getting away. The girls didn't
want to lose sight of them! "Florence,
would you be able to turn us into fairies?"
Kirsty asked, thinking fast. "That way we
can fly after the goblins."

"Good idea," Florence said, pointing
her wand at the girls and muttering some
magical-sounding words.

Instantly, a stream of bright sparkles flew out from her wand and swirled all around Kirsty and Rachel. And then, moments later, they were shrinking smaller and smaller…and they had their own shining fairy wings on their backs. Even Kirsty's shopping bag had shrunk down to fairy-size!

Luckily, nobody was around to see them as the three fairies flew up into the air and began zooming after the goblin gang.

"We need a plan," Rachel said thoughtfully. They could see in the distance that the goblins had reached the row of shops and had slowed down, obviously thinking they'd got away from the fairies.

"If we could somehow just get that small goblin to drop the book..." Kirsty said, thinking aloud. "Maybe if we can make him jump, he might let go of it..."

"And then I could magic it back to fairy-size and fly in to grab it!" Florence finished.

The three friends smiled at one another. "We could fly up behind them so that we're really close to them," Rachel

suggested, "then Florence could turn us
back into girls, and we could shout really
loudly. That should make them jump!"

Kirsty giggled. "It would make *me*
jump," she said. "Come on, let's try it."

Silently, the fairies flew as close to the
goblins as they dared. Luckily, the goblins
had their backs turned to peer into the
sweet shop, moaning that there weren't
any 'bogmallows' in there. When Kirsty
and Rachel were hovering just behind

the goblin holding Florence's memory book, Florence waved her wand, turning them back into girls.

"BOOOOO!" Rachel and Kirsty shouted at the tops of their voices.

"Aarrrgh!" screamed the goblins, turning round in fright…but unfortunately, the smallest goblin didn't drop the book as they'd hoped. In fact, he only clutched it tighter…and all of the goblins ran away up the street once more!

A Tempting Offer

"After them!" cried Florence, whizzing through the air like a streak of light. Kirsty and Rachel followed, running as fast as they could.

The goblins ducked down an alleyway, with Florence and the girls right behind. Kirsty grinned as she realised something – the alley was a dead end. Soon the goblins would be trapped!

Sure enough, moments later, the goblins realised there was nowhere else to run. They stopped and turned, their backs against the wall. The smallest goblin hid the memory book behind him, a determined glint in his eye. "You're not getting this back," he said sullenly.

"I don't know why you want *my* memory book anyway," Florence said. "You goblins hate pink, sparkly things. Wouldn't you rather have a nice green memory book of your own?"

"Well, yes, but…" the tallest goblin said, shrugging. "We haven't got one, have we? So we're having yours instead."

This gave Rachel an idea. "But maybe if we could find you the perfect goblin memory book, with a gorgeous green cover, you might…swap?" she suggested, crossing her fingers behind her back.

The goblins looked at one another but none of them spoke.

Kirsty tried to hide her smile. It was obvious they *did* want their own book!

"Florence, would you be able to magic up a new memory book for the goblins?" she asked.

"Of course!" Florence said. "I could make you one just how you wanted. Maybe the cover could have prickly bits on, or slimy patches…"

"Oooh!" the goblins chorused, eyes lighting up.

"I'd make the pages green, too,"
Florence went on temptingly. "And I'd
even add some special magic so that
you can add your favourite *smells* to the
book… IF you give me my book back."

"Favourite *smells*," the knobbly-kneed
goblin said longingly. "We could put in
the smell of mouldy toadstools."

"And smelly feet!" another suggested.

They all looked at each other. "It's a
deal!" they chorused.

"Hooray!" cheered Kirsty, Rachel and
Florence. Then Florence set to work. She
waved her wand and muttered some
magical words. Seconds later, a big green
book appeared in the tallest goblin's
hands with a squelch. It was oozing with
some yucky-smelling slime, and had a
sticky, prickly cover.

"Oh," said the tallest goblin, stroking it.
"It's so ugly…it's perfect!" He turned to
the smallest goblin. "Go on, hand it over,"
he ordered. "This is worth *fifty* silly fairy
memory books!"

The smallest goblin thrust out Florence's
memory book. With a smile of delight,
she waved her wand, and it shrank to
its Fairyland size on the goblin's palm.
Then she fluttered down and picked it up.

"Thank you," she said happily.

The goblins wandered off, excitedly discussing what smells they'd add to their new book and how Jack Frost would love their horrid handiwork.

"Take your time," Florence called after them. "Memory books, like true friendships, can't be rushed!" Then she smiled at Kirsty and Rachel. "And now to repair my memory book – and all the others that have been spoiled!"

She touched her wand to her memory book and bright, shimmering waves of magic began to pulse from it, spreading through the air in sparkling ripples of light.

"There," she said happily, as the last one flickered and disappeared. "All should be well once more and your memory book will be full again." She smiled. "Thanks, both of you," she said, fluttering over to give them tiny fairy kisses. "I'd better go back to Fairyland now, to finish getting everything ready for tomorrow's Friendship Day. See you soon, I hope. Oh, and maybe you should have a look in that shopping bag?"

"In the shopping bag?" Kirsty asked, glancing down at the empty canvas bag that still hung from her arm.

"Byeeee!" called Florence mischievously, vanishing into the distance.

Kirsty opened the bag and peered inside. Then she smiled.

"What is it?" Rachel asked, trying to see.

Kirsty pulled out two pink invitations with their names written in silver ink. *"You are invited to the fairies' Friendship Day at the Fairyland Palace,"* she read, beaming. "Oh, Rachel! How exciting!"

"Brilliant!" Rachel cheered, hugging Kirsty happily. She grinned as they began walking towards the shops. "I knew this was going to be another good holiday together, Kirsty. I just knew it!"

The Friendship Ribbon

Contents

Party Preparations   61

Off to Fairyland   69

Goblin Games   79

Ribbons for Racing   89

Party Time!   97

Party Preparations

"Good morning, everyone!" Mrs Tate said, smiling around the hall. "And thank you so much for offering to lend a hand. There's a lot to do!"

It was the following day, and Kirsty and Rachel had come to the village hall with Kirsty's mum and a group of villagers to help with preparations for the grand reopening party.

The hall had recently been redecorated, with the whole community pitching in to help, and was being renamed 'The Wetherbury Friendship Hall'.

"We have balloons, streamers and bunting to sort through and hang up," Mrs Tate said, "the music system to organise, fairy lights to arrange... Oh, and my banner! Kirsty and Rachel, would you help me unroll it, please?"

Rachel, Kirsty and her mum carefully unrolled the large white banner, until everyone could see what was written on it: WELCOME TO THE WETHERBURY FRIENDSHIP HALL!

"It doesn't look very exciting at the moment, but I've brought along a selection of different coloured paints," Mrs Tate went on. "And as this party is all about friendship and working together, I thought it would be nice if lots of different people could paint a letter of the banner each," she explained. "That way, it'll look really bright and eye-catching. OK? Let's get started!"

The team of helpers immediately set to work – some blowing up balloons, others untangling the long strings of bunting and ropes of fairy lights from their boxes.

"Shall we paint our letters on the banner first?" Kirsty asked Rachel.

"Good idea," Rachel said. "Let's take it into one of the side rooms, so it won't get in people's way."

The girls carried the banner and paints into a smaller room off the main hall, which had a piano at one end, and lots of chairs stacked up in towers. They spread the banner out on the floor, then chose their paints and brushes. Kirsty took the pink paint while Rachel decided on purple, and then both girls carefully filled

in a letter each.

"This is going to look great when everyone's painted their letters," Rachel said, admiring their work.

"Definitely," said Kirsty with a smile. She was just about to go and wash her paintbrush when she heard a tiny sigh of relief from behind her.

"There you are!" came a familiar silvery voice. "I'm so glad to see you both. Kirsty, Rachel, I really need your help again!"

Both girls turned to see Florence flying through an open window, her pretty face looking pale and anxious. "What's happened?" Rachel asked. "Are you OK?"

Florence fluttered down to land on the
pot of green paint, her wings drooping.
"No, not really," she said sadly. "It's the
fairies' Friendship Party later on today
but everything is going wrong...and it's
the goblins' fault again! They've run off
with my friendship ribbon and if I don't
get it back, the party will be a disaster!
Please would you come to Fairyland with
me, and help look for it?"

"Of course!" Kirsty said at once. Then she bit her lip. "The only thing is, we're meant to be helping my mum here."

"Don't worry," Florence said. "I can work some magic so that time will stand still in the human world while you're with me in Fairyland. Is that all right?"

Rachel nodded, her eyes lighting up at the thought of another fairy adventure. "Brilliant," she replied.

Florence smiled. "Then let's go – there's no time to lose!"

Off to Fairyland

Florence waved her wand and a stream
of pink and purple sparkles swirled all
around Rachel and Kirsty, lifting them
off the ground in a glittering whirlwind.
The room became a blur of colours
before their eyes and they felt themselves
spinning through the air, growing smaller
and smaller and smaller...

A few moments later, they felt their feet touch down on the ground, and the sparkly whirlwind slowed and vanished. Kirsty realised they were in the grounds of the palace, and lots of fairies she recognised were busily working away. They were back in Fairyland – and they were fairies, too, with their own shimmering wings!

Rachel beamed at Kirsty. Fairyland was the most exciting place *ever*!

"Look, there's Polly the Party Fun Fairy," she said, pointing as she spotted the little blonde fairy across the courtyard. "Oh, and Melodie the Music Fairy, too."

Polly appeared to be working on a new party game which involved teams of fairies competing to fly up and collect glittering golden stars from a nearby tree, while Melodie was listening to the Fairyland orchestra rehearse, but both seemed to be having problems.

Florence bit her lip anxiously as Polly's fairies bumped into each other in mid-air and crashed to the ground with surprised shouts, and Melodie put her head in her hands at the squeaks and squawks the musicians were making.

"Oh dear," sighed Florence. "Things are still no better here. We've got to find that friendship ribbon! Without that, the party is going to be awful."

"What *is* the friendship ribbon?" Kirsty asked, confused.

Florence opened her mouth to reply but then gave a shout of warning instead. "Phoebe! Look out!"

Rachel and Kirsty turned to see Phoebe the Fashion Fairy pushing a rail of gorgeous party dresses along a cobbled path a short distance away. The clothes rail was bouncing and jolting on the cobbles, and several of the dresses and accessories had slipped off their hangers onto the ground without Phoebe realising.

Phoebe turned at Florence's shout and spotted the fallen items, but before she could pick them up, Zoe the Skating Fairy whizzed up behind her carrying a huge box...and rollerskated right over the dresses, completely ruining them!

"Oh no!" wailed Phoebe in dismay. "My dresses!"

Zoe skidded around to see what had happened, and threw up her hands in horror...

dropping the box which landed with a crash. "Oh no!" she echoed.

"Your dresses – and the best royal china plates!"

Florence looked as if she wanted to cry. "This is getting worse and worse!" she said. She turned back to Kirsty and Rachel. "The friendship ribbon is always tied to the maypole," she explained, pointing to where a tall golden pole stood in the centre of a neat lawn.

The three fairies fluttered over to it.
"While it's there, it means that friends
can work harmoniously, and have the
best fun together. It was going to be used
in a special friendship dance around the
maypole tonight, but unfortunately the
goblins saw the ribbon and decided *they*
wanted to play with it. And ever since

they took it down, things have been going wrong."

"We'll help you find the ribbon," Rachel promised her. "Come on, let's start looking for it – and those sneaky goblins, too!"

Goblin Games

Florence, Kirsty and Rachel fluttered up into the air and flew above the palace grounds, keeping a lookout for any signs of goblins below. They passed the bakery, where it smelled as if something was burning horribly, then flew over the party decoration workshop.

Grace the Glitter Fairy had just accidentally knocked over a huge barrel of sequins which poured out in a twinkling flood all over the floor. "Oh, *no!*" they heard her cry in exasperation. According to Florence, the friendship ribbon was long, bright blue and covered in stars, but as the three friends flew past the palace stables and across the lake, there was no sign of it – or the goblins – anywhere.

"Let's try looking in here," Florence suggested, pointing to a small wooded area ahead. Kirsty and Rachel followed as she swooped between the shady trees.

Birds sang sweetly and a light breeze
rustled the leaves as the three fairies
flew through the wood. Then Florence
landed abruptly and turned,
putting a finger to her
lips, before ducking
behind a large tree
trunk.

Rachel and Kirsty
could hear muffled shouts
and cheers, and hurried to
hide behind trees of their own
as they realised that there was a group
of six goblins gathered in a clearing a
little way ahead. Peering around their
trees, they could see that the goblins were
playing with the ribbon – using it as a
sparkly skipping rope at first, and then
as a rope for a tug-of-war game.

Florence's eyes were wide with alarm.
"They'd better not rip it!" she murmured.
"I can't bear to watch!"

The goblins were split into two teams
of three for the tug-of-war, and
eventually, one team pulled the others
over a branch on the ground that they
were using as a marker. "We win!" cried
the tallest goblin on the winning team,
letting go of the ribbon to celebrate with

his team mates. Then he taunted the others. "Losers! Losers!"

"Your team *cheated!*" argued a sullen-faced goblin, putting his hands on his hips. "That's not fair. I don't want to be friends with you any more."

The two goblins started fighting, and another goblin had to break them up. "Hey, stop that, this is meant to be our friendship party," he reminded them. "Anything the stupid fairies can do, we can do better – right?"

"Right," muttered the tall goblin sulkily.

"How about a game of blind goblin's buff?" the smallest goblin suggested. "We can use the ribbon as a blindfold."

Florence beckoned Kirsty and Rachel behind a sprawling shrub while the goblins began arguing over who was going to be the 'blind goblin' first. "I really need to get that ribbon from them," she whispered, "but I don't know how we'll manage it, when they keep using it in all their games."

Kirsty nodded. "They're really enjoying playing with it, aren't they?" she murmured.

She watched as the smallest goblin
ended the argument about who would
be blindfolded first by tying the ribbon
quickly around his own head. The other
goblins dodged away from him, giggling
as he blundered about, arms outstretched,
trying to catch one of them.

Being goblins, however, they didn't
play nicely for very long. One of them
picked up a twig and used it to jab the
blindfolded goblin in the ribs.

"Ow!" he yelped, and flailed his fists around, causing the others to crack up laughing.

Then another of the goblins threw a handful of acorns at the blindfolded one, causing him to cry out in surprise as they pinged off his pointy nose. "Stop it!" he yelled, running towards the noise of their cackles. "Stop it!"

Rachel, Kirsty and Florence, meanwhile, were still trying to come up with a plan to get the ribbon, but it was hard to think straight, with the noise of the squabbling goblins in the background. Then Kirsty smiled. "I've got an idea!" she whispered.

Ribbons for Racing

"Florence, would you be able to magic up some other ribbons that look the same as the friendship ribbon?" Kirsty asked.

Florence nodded. "Of course," she said. "They won't be quite as sparkly as the friendship ribbon, but—"

"That's fine," Kirsty said, interrupting in her eagerness. "In fact, that's perfect!

Let's tell the goblins that the only way to
see who are the best friends is to hold a
three-legged race. We can use the ribbons
to tie up their legs, and then hopefully
they'll be so distracted by the race that
we'll be able to sneak up and take the
friendship ribbon, and fly off!"

Florence grinned.
"I love it!" she
said. She
waved her
wand and
muttered
some magic
words under
her breath and
then, in a swirl
of pink sparkles, two
matching ribbons appeared in her hand.

"There!" she smiled. "Now, let's put our plan into action."

Rachel, Kirsty and Florence all fluttered into the clearing, just as the smallest goblin ripped off his blindfold. "I'm not playing this game any more," he said crossly. "You lot are so mean! You're the worst friends ever!"

"Oh dear," Rachel said solemnly. "Worst friends ever? That's not good. We were just wondering which of you are *best* friends."

The goblins all replied at once. "I'm best friends with him, but he likes *him* better than me."

"I don't like him or him or him, but
he's OK, I suppose."

"I'm the best at everything, so I must
be the best friend," another boasted.

"Well," Kirsty said loudly, over their
chatter, "how do you fancy having a race,
to decide who are the best friends of all?
We've got some extra ribbons here, so you
can have a three-legged race. Get into
pairs as quickly as you can!"

Kirsty spoke so firmly that the goblins
all scurried to find a partner and tie their
legs together.

"The first pair to the weeping willow tree wins!" Rachel said. "Ready, steady... go!"

The goblins began hobbling off in their pairs, all looking very determined. But as they ran, Kirsty began to feel doubtful that her plan would work. They were actually all really good at running three-legged! Would *any* of them fall over?

"Hmmm," said Florence, as if reading Kirsty's mind. "Maybe I should make things a bit trickier for them..." She waved her wand and muttered some more magic words. A stream of sparkles swirled out from her wand, and suddenly, lots of stones and acorns rolled in front of the goblins' feet!

"Ooh! Ahh!" wailed the goblins as, one by one, they stumbled and tripped on top of each other!

They weren't hurt, but the goblins were soon in a tangle of arms and legs, all shouting and arguing.

"Quick!" Rachel urged. "Now's our chance to get the ribbon!"

Party Time!

Florence didn't need telling twice! She zoomed through the air and deftly untied the sparkliest ribbon from the tangle of goblin legs, then fluttered up high. "Got it!" she cheered. "Come on, let's fly back and tie it to the maypole!"

Rachel and Kirsty soared into the air after Florence and the three of them flew all the way back to the palace grounds, where Florence tied the ribbon back on the maypole. "Hurrah!" they cheered, hugging each other in triumph.

"Is that Kirsty and Rachel I see?" came a booming voice. The girls turned to see the Fairy King and Queen walking into the courtyard area, with big smiles on their faces.

Rachel and Kirsty smiled back politely and bobbed curtseys.

King Oberon and Queen Titania were always really lovely, but the girls still felt rather shy in front of them. "Hello," they chorused.

Florence flew down from the maypole. "Kirsty and Rachel have helped me twice in the last two days, Your Majesties," she said. "Yesterday they helped me get my magic memory book from the goblins, and today they helped rescue the friendship ribbon. They are true friends to the fairies indeed!"

Queen Titania smiled. "In that case, girls, we would be very honoured if you two could declare our Friendship Party officially open," she said. She waved her wand and there came the sound of a bell ringing majestically. All the fairies in the area fell silent and turned to see what was happening.

Holding hands, Rachel and Kirsty looked at each other and then said in the same breath, "We declare the fairy

Friendship Party officially...OPEN!"

A great cheer went up as the celebrations began. Melodie and her orchestra played some beautiful music, while another group of fairies performed their special friendship dance around the maypole. Then everyone went into the Great Hall of the palace, which Grace the Glitter Fairy had decorated with the most wonderful pink and silver streamers, for some party games with Polly.

Rachel and Kirsty had a fantastic time! Polly's new party games were such fun. They played Best Friend Hide and Seek, joined in some flying obstacle races and a treasure hunt, and then took part in a Best Friend Fun Quiz. It was lovely to see so many of their fairy friends again, with everyone enjoying themselves.

A little later, Cherry the Cake Fairy and Honey the Sweet Fairy made all sorts of delicious food appear. Kirsty and Rachel tucked into Cherry's delicious Rose and Lavender Cupcakes, and Honey's Fairy Fizz-drops and Magic Marshmallow Melts.

"Delicious,"

Kirsty said, licking her lips. "Thank you, Honey, those are the yummiest sweets I've ever tasted!"

"And the nicest, fluffiest cakes too," Rachel said, smiling at Cherry. "What a great Friendship Party this is!"

King Oberon and Queen Titania appeared beside the girls. "Thanks again for everything you've done for the fairies," the king said. "I'm afraid we need to send you back to your world now, but I hope you'll be back before too long."

Florence flew over to say goodbye.

"Thanks from me, too," she said. "It's
wonderful to be friends with you!"

"It's wonderful to be friends with *all*
of you," Kirsty replied, her eyes shining.

"See you soon, I hope," Rachel said,
as the queen pointed her wand at them,
and muttered a magic command.

Golden fairy dust
billowed out,
spinning around
the girls and
whisking
them away
in a glittering
whirlwind.
Seconds later,
they were back in the
village hall, by the banner and paints. But
something was different.

"Look, Kirsty!" Rachel whispered in delight. She pointed at the letters they'd painted on the banner, and Kirsty's eyes widened. The pink letter she'd painted was now edged with shining golden paint, and Rachel's purple letter had been patterned with tiny silver hearts.

"Fairy magic," Kirsty said with a smile. "Don't they look pretty?"

Just at that moment, Mrs Tate came
into the room. "Well done, girls," she said,
when she saw they'd been painting. Then
she took a closer look. "Goodness!" she
exclaimed. "They are beautiful, you've
done such a great job!"

Rachel and Kirsty exchanged a secret smile. They knew they couldn't take all the credit for the letters. Fairy magic had made them extra-special – but the two friends weren't about to tell Mrs Tate that!

The Friendship
Bracelets

Contents

Village Celebrations   113

Florence Flies In!   121

That's Magic!   131

Tricks...and Treasure!   141

The Hunt Is On   153

Village Celebrations

"Hold still… There," said Kirsty Tate, zipping up her best friend Rachel Walker's dress.

"Thanks," Rachel smiled. "I'm really looking forward to this party, Kirsty!"

The two girls were in Kirsty's bedroom, getting ready for a special celebration in Wetherbury, the village where Kirsty lived.

A year ago, the Wetherbury Village Hall had had to close because it needed lots of repairs. Since then, a team of villagers had worked hard, rebuilding parts of the hall, putting on a new roof and decorating it from top to bottom. Now, at last, it was finished, and had been renamed the 'Wetherbury Friendship Hall' to celebrate the great teamwork that had gone into it.

Kirsty's mum had helped organise a big party for the villagers and all their friends that evening, to mark the hall's reopening.

Rachel and her family had come to
stay with the Tates for the weekend, so
they were going to the party, too. And,
best of all, Rachel and Kirsty were in
the middle of another fairy adventure!
Florence the Friendship Fairy looked after
happy times and special friendships in
both Fairyland and the human world, but,
as usual, mean Jack Frost and his goblins
were determined to spoil things.

So far, the girls had helped Florence the
Friendship Fairy get her
magical memory
book and her
friendship ribbon
back, after these
had been stolen
by the naughty
goblins.

The party was in full swing when Kirsty and Rachel and their families arrived at the hall. The girls had helped decorate the main room and it looked wonderful, with pink and red streamers and matching balloons. Rachel and Kirsty knew there would be lots of games later, a treasure hunt, a barbecue and even a magician!

"Wow, this is great," Rachel said.

"It is," Kirsty agreed. "But nobody seems to be enjoying themselves. I wonder why?"

Rachel looked closer. To her surprise, she could see sour expressions on some children's faces. Nearby, some boys glared at each other. "There's no way Liverpool are better than Chelsea," one snarled.

"You don't know what you're talking about!" Elsewhere, other children with sulky faces sat on the chairs lining the room, not speaking to anyone.

Mr and Mrs Tate didn't seem to notice, and took Rachel's parents off to introduce them to some other friends, but Kirsty and Rachel remained hovering at the edge of the party, wondering what was going on. "I've got the feeling that something is wrong," Kirsty said.

"It's awful, isn't it?" came a tinkling voice from behind them. "I'm so glad you're here!"

Florence Flies In!

Kirsty and Rachel turned to see a
tiny fairy peeping out from one of the
balloons. It was Florence the Friendship
Fairy!

"Hello again, girls," she said, "I'm
afraid I need your help one more time."
Her shoulders drooped and she suddenly
looked upset. "I think it's all my fault that
people are breaking friends at this party!"

"I'm sure it's not," Kirsty said, feeling very sorry for Florence. "Why don't we go somewhere quieter, and you can tell us what happened?"

Florence agreed and fluttered under Kirsty's hair so that she would stay hidden. The girls went outside and down the side of the hall where nobody was around.

Florence flitted out from her hiding place and perched on some ivy growing up the wall. "Well, you've helped me so much over the last couple of days," she began, "and I know just how many times you've helped the other fairies too, in one way or another. We all really value your friendship."

Rachel felt pleased. "Well, we love being friends with you all, too," she said.

Florence smiled. "I'm glad to hear it," she said. "And I wanted to give you each a special friendship bracelet as gifts, to say thank you. So, after our Friendship Party last night, I asked the Rainbow Fairies to contribute strands of colour to the bracelets. When I had the seven colours of the rainbow, I added an extra thread of gold which was full of my special friendship magic, then wove them all together into two bracelets."

"How lovely!" Kirsty exclaimed.

Florence's face fell. "They were lovely," she replied. "I even worked in some extra special wish-magic that would grant you both a wish when you were wearing the bracelets. But unfortunately, Jack Frost overheard me telling the Rainbow Fairies about my plans. I'm sorry to say he didn't want you to have the bracelets, so he ordered his goblins to steal them from my workshop."

"How mean!" Rachel said. "Why doesn't he want us to have them?"

"Perhaps he wanted to punish you, because you helped me get the memory book and the friendship ribbon back from his goblins," Florence said sadly. "And you know how cold and spiky he is. He doesn't understand friendship, or wanting to do nice things for other people. He doesn't exactly have many friends himself."

"That's true," Kirsty said thoughtfully. Jack Frost had lots of goblin servants, but you couldn't call them friends. "So, does Jack Frost have the bracelets now?"

"No," Florence said. "Those goblins are so sneaky, they decided to have some fun before they took the bracelets to their master. They heard about this party, and didn't want to miss out, so they came along. And that's the problem."

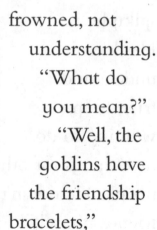

Rachel frowned, not understanding. "What do you mean?"

"Well, the goblins have the friendship bracelets,"

Florence went on. "But they don't realise that a friendship bracelet should only be worn by the person it was made for.

If someone else wears it, my friendship magic works in reverse, causing the wearer, and anyone near the wearer, to start arguing and breaking friends."

"So that's why we saw people arguing earlier," Kirsty realised. "By stealing our bracelets and coming here with them, the goblins are causing everyone to break friends!"

"Exactly," Florence replied. "And I've got to stop them before they spoil the whole party. Will you help me find them, and get the bracelets back?"

"Of course," Rachel said. "Let's start looking!"

The three friends went back into the
hall. People were dancing, and Kirsty
and Rachel peered closely at them. Some
children had put on fancy dress costumes
for the occasion, and with the dancefloor
so busy, it was difficult to make out
everybody's faces.

Just then Rachel noticed two boys
heading onto the dancefloor, bickering
loudly.

They were both in fancy dress – one as a pirate, the other as a knight, but there was no mistaking their long noses and pointy ears. They were goblins!

That's Magic!

"There they are!" Rachel hissed, pointing at the goblins as they stomped across the room. They were bickering about who was the best dancer, and both started dancing as if to prove that they were better, whilst still looking very bad-tempered.

All around the goblins new arguments began springing up – and what silly arguments they were! "Short hair is better than long hair," one girl snapped at another, who had a long plait. "I don't want to be friends with anyone with long hair."

"I don't like your T-shirt – so I don't like you!" one boy muttered to another.

"This is getting worse by the minute,"

Florence groaned. "I'm going to try sprinkling some friendship magic around in the hope that it'll patch up these arguments."

Kirsty and Rachel watched as Florence flew high up in the air. They saw her wave her wand, and then streams of pink stars swirled into the room.

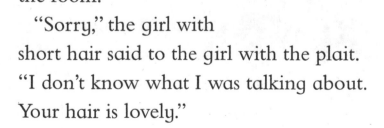

"Sorry," the girl with short hair said to the girl with the plait. "I don't know what I was talking about. Your hair is lovely."

"I didn't mean to be rude about your T-shirt," the boy said, returning to his friend. "Shall we go outside and play?"

"Florence's magic is working!" Kirsty said happily.

"But so is the magic from the bracelets," Rachel said. "Look!"

It was true. As fast as Florence helped people make friends, new arguments started up elsewhere. The two goblins were still bickering. Then, as the pirate goblin shoved the knight, the sleeve

of his pirate shirt rode up – and Kirsty noticed a rainbow-coloured bracelet on his wrist. Aha!

"There's one of the bracelets," she whispered to Rachel. "But how can we get it back?"

Before Rachel could reply, the singer of the band finished his song. "We're going to take a break now, but there's a very special guest who'll be entertaining you while we're away. Here's...Milo the Magician!"

A big "Ooooh!" of excitement went up as a man in a cloak and top hat walked onstage.

Everyone hurried to fetch a chair
and then sat down to watch the show,
including the goblins. Rachel and Kirsty
sat down at the back of the hall, with
Florence hidden under Kirsty's hair.

"There!" Florence hissed suddenly,
pointing. Kirsty and Rachel leaned
forward and counted one, two, THREE
goblins sitting in the front row. One wore
the pirate costume, one the knight outfit,
and the third wore a tall wizard's hat
and cloak.

"Oh, no," Rachel said. "Three goblins and two bracelets – this could get tricky."

The magician's show began, and the girls watched with interest. He plucked oranges from behind people's ears and produced a rabbit from his hat. Kirsty and Rachel thought he was great, but unfortunately the children in the audience were sulky and restless, glaring at one another. The goblins all seemed to enjoy the tricks though, and clapped enthusiastically throughout.

When Milo's show ended, Mrs Tate
came on to the stage. "We're going to
start a game of hide and seek now, in the
garden," she said. "Follow me, everyone!"

Most people – including the pirate and
the knight goblins – hurried after Kirsty's
mum, but the goblin with the wizard's
hat stayed where he was. "I want more
magic!" he said to Milo, who was packing
up his equipment.

"Sorry," Milo said. "Show's over – even
for wizards. Why don't you go outside
with the others?"

The goblin didn't budge. "I want more magic," he repeated. As he did so, the girls spotted a brightly coloured stripe on one of his wrists – the second friendship bracelet!

"I've got an idea," Kirsty said excitedly. "If the goblin wants a magic show, maybe we could give him one. And then we could use some real magic to get the bracelet off him!"

Florence grinned. "Let's give it a go!" she said.

Tricks...and Treasure!

Milo left the hall, and the goblin stayed right where he was, glaring into space. "Perfect," Florence said. "It's time for us to put on our very own show."

Florence waved her wand and the girls were suddenly wearing magician-style costumes of capes, hats and wands!

"Hi," Rachel said, strolling around in front of the goblin. "Like magic, do you? Want to see another show?"

The goblin blinked in surprise. "Where did you come from?" he asked.

Kirsty tapped her nose mysteriously as she walked to join Rachel. "Magic," she said. "Now let's see…what's this egg doing here?"

She reached behind the goblin's pointy right ear and hoped with all her heart that Florence would be able to help her with the trick! Yes – a smooth egg appeared in her palm at just the right moment, and she drew her hand back to show the goblin what was in it.

"Goodness!" Rachel said, trying not to laugh at the goblin's startled expression. "Didn't your parents ever teach you to wash behind your ears?

"Do some more, do some more!" the goblin urged. "More magic!"

Kirsty pulled off her top hat, and showed the goblin that it was empty. "Nothing in there, right?" she said. "But let's see what happens when I say the magic words... *Bibble Bobble Bibble Bobble!*"

The goblin gasped – and so did Kirsty.
As she finished bibble-bobbling, a
beautiful white dove flew straight out
of her hat, and through
the open
window.

"Whoa!"
the goblin
cried.
"You're
even
better than
Milo!"
"And now
for another trick," Rachel announced.
"This may look like an ordinary wand,"
she said, tapping it against the goblin's
wizard hat, "but if I throw it up in
the air and catch it, it turns into…"

She held her breath and threw the wand
up high. There was a pink sparkle of
magic dust, and then a string of colourful
silk handkerchiefs shot out from the
end of the wand…and started to wrap
themselves tightly around the goblin!

"Oooh!" the goblin cried. "That was
good."

Kirsty and Rachel watched as the
handkerchiefs wound round and round
the goblin. Soon he could no longer
clap, as his arms were bound tight to his
body. And then the excited light vanished
from his eyes. "Hey!" he said. "What's
happening?"

"*This!*" replied Kirsty, as she quickly untied the friendship bracelet from his wrist. "Thank you very much!"

The goblin's mouth fell open as he realised he'd been tricked. "You... You..." he stuttered. "You horrible magicians! That's not fair!"

"*I* didn't think it was very fair either, when you and your friends stole my bracelets," Florence said, flying down and landing on Rachel's shoulder.

The goblin made a furious growling noise and stumbled off. "I'll make sure you don't get the other one, anyway," he called. "So there!"

Kirsty and Rachel admired the friendship bracelet in Kirsty's hands. It had 'Kirsty' stitched along it in tiny golden letters. "Here, let me put it on for you," Florence said with a smile. She waved her wand, making both magician costumes vanish – and the bracelet tied itself neatly around Kirsty's wrist. "Ta-da!"

"It's beautiful," Kirsty said happily.
"Thank you so much,
Florence. Now
we just need to
get Rachel's
bracelet."

"Let's go and
see what those
goblins are up
to," Florence said.
She hid in the front
pocket of Rachel's bag,
and the girls set off.

As they went outside, they almost ran
straight into the goblins. The wizard
goblin had been untied and they all
looked very smug. "Come for the bracelet,
have you?" the knight goblin said. "Ha!
You'll never find it now."

"Yeah," the pirate goblin gloated, showing them his bare wrists. "We've hidden it somewhere really good."

"Listen, everyone!" called Kirsty's mum just then. "While the grown-ups light the barbecue, there's going to be a treasure hunt. There's real treasure at the end, in an actual treasure chest!"

The goblins looked at each other in horror. "What… What does the treasure chest look like?" the pirate goblin croaked after a moment.

"It's a small golden box," Mrs Tate replied.

The goblins all looked utterly dismayed about something. Rachel elbowed Kirsty.

"I bet they've hidden the bracelet in the treasure chest!" she guessed. "And that's why they look so worried!"

"I think you're right," Kirsty said excitedly. "So we've got to find that treasure chest before they do!"

The Hunt Is On

"Here's the first clue," Mrs Tate continued.
"Use two sticks to tap on my skin,
I make a bang – some call it a din!"

Kirsty solved the clue very quickly.
"Two sticks to tap on my skin... It's
a drum," she whispered to Rachel. "It
must be the drum that the band used.
Come on!"

Kirsty and Rachel began running towards the hall.

"We've got to get to the treasure chest first so we can take the bracelet out before anyone else sees it," Rachel panted as they ran. "But how are we going to manage that?"

"By flying, of course," Florence said, popping her head out of Rachel's bag. "Find somewhere quiet, and I'll turn you both into fairies!"

Kirsty immediately veered away from
the stage and ducked into the bathroom.
Florence waved her wand, sending more
of her glittering fairy
dust spinning all
around them.
Seconds later,
they were
fairies! They
fluttered
their wings
and flew
back into
the hall, just in
time to hear a boy
reading aloud the second clue.

"We're bright and colourful, and filled
with air. Tied to a string, the next clue is
there…" he said, frowning.

"Bright and colourful? Sounds like flowers," one girl said eagerly.

Kirsty, Rachel and Florence, who were now perched on one of the ceiling beams, exchanged smiles. "Balloons!" they all said together. "Quick!"

They soared out into the garden. There was a big bunch of balloons tied to a tree, and they swooped down to land in the middle of them. The clue was attached to the string of one of the balloons. This clue led them to the front door of the hall, and they spotted a large metal

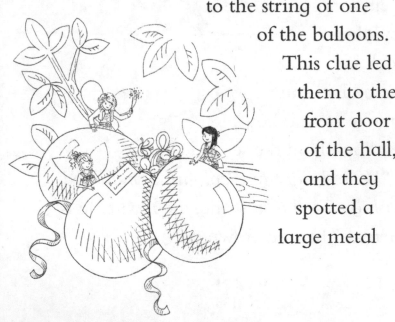

letterbox attached to the inside of the door…and what was that, poking out of it?

"It's the treasure chest!" Rachel cheered excitedly.

Kirsty opened the letterbox flap and then opened the golden chest. Sure enough, lying on top of a pile of chocolate coins, there was a second friendship bracelet, this one with 'Rachel' embroidered on it.

"It's gorgeous," Rachel exclaimed, taking it out. "Thank you, Florence!"

"My pleasure," Florence replied, waving her wand and returning the girls to human-size. The bracelet magically tied itself around Rachel's wrist.

Suddenly, they heard footsteps approaching. "Sounds like the other party-goers are on their way – quick, out of the front door!" Florence urged.

Kirsty closed the treasure chest, then she and Rachel ran in a loop around the building and back through the hall, with Florence hiding in Rachel's bag. They couldn't let anyone know that they'd found the treasure first!

They reached the front porch again just in time to hear cheers from the other children who were gathered by the front door. "Chocolate coins!" someone whooped. "Yummy!"

Rachel had assumed that now she'd got her bracelet, everyone would go back to being friends, but it didn't seem to have worked like that.

The children by the door – and the goblins! – were pushing and shoving each other to snatch up chocolate coins, even though there were plenty to go around.

"Do you remember me saying that I added some special wish magic to your bracelets when I made them?" Florence said quietly. "Well, now you can make your wish."

Kirsty's eyes lit up with excitement, as did Rachel's. What should they wish for?

"As these are friendship bracelets, maybe we should make a wish of friendship?" Rachel said after a moment.

"Yes, for everyone here," Kirsty suggested.

Florence beamed. "I couldn't have put it better myself," she said.

Kirsty and Rachel held hands. "We wish that everyone could be friends again!" they chorused.

Both girls felt their wrists tingle and lots of sparkly magic flew up into the air. And then…

"Sorry I wasn't very nice to you earlier," one boy said to another. "It's cool that we support different football teams – it doesn't mean we can't be friends."

"I like pink *and* purple," one girl said to the girl next to her. "But I like being friends with you much more than *any* colour!"

"That's more like it," Florence said happily.

Just then, one of the grown-ups shouted that the barbecue was ready, and the children ran outside, laughing and joking. Only the goblins were left – and they didn't look quite so happy.

"Cheer up," Florence told them. "Here – let me make you your own friendship bracelets." She waved her wand and three bracelets appeared on the goblins' wrists.

They weren't quite as special-looking as Rachel and Kirsty's bracelets, but the goblins looked very pleased.

"And here's one to take home to Jack Frost," Florence said, magicking up a silvery-white bracelet and handing it to the nearest goblin. "Hopefully this will help him become a good friend to others. Maybe even to the fairies!"

The goblins thanked her politely and went off, all being extra-nice to each other. "You're the ugliest goblin I've ever seen," the pirate goblin said kindly to the wizard goblin.

"Oh, thank you!" the wizard goblin replied, blushing. "But you definitely have the pointiest nose!"

It was all Rachel and Kirsty could do not to burst out laughing. They'd never seen the goblins being so friendly – even if they did have a strange idea about compliments!

"It's been lovely to meet you," Florence said, "thank you so much for all your help! I'd better return to Fairyland now. I'm sure the rest of the party will be great fun, now that everyone is friends again."

"Thanks, Florence," Kirsty said. "I love my bracelet – and I love being friends with the fairies!"

"Me too," Rachel said.

"See you soon, I hope."

Florence blew them a kiss and fluttered away, and Kirsty and Rachel rejoined the party-goers. Everyone was very jolly, and there was lots of laughter and happy conversation.

"Hooray for friends," Kirsty said, slipping an arm through Rachel's.

Kirsty smiled. "And hooray for fairies, too!" she said. "I hope we have lots more adventures together!"

Now it's time for Kirsty and Rachel
to help...

Madison the Magic Show Fairy

Read on for a sneak peek...

Rachel Walker gazed excitedly out of
the car window, as her mum parked.
A short distance away she could see a
helter-skelter, a spinning tea-cups ride,
the dodgems, and all sorts of sideshows
and stalls. "This is going to be fun!" she
said to her best friend, Kirsty Tate, who
was sitting next to her in the back seat.

Kirsty grinned. "It looks great," she
said, her eyes shining. Kirsty had come to
stay at Rachel's house for a whole week
during the October half-term, and it was
lovely to be with Rachel again. The
girls always had the best time when they

were together…and the most exciting fairy adventures, too! They had helped the fairies in many different ways before, although their parents and other friends had no idea about their amazing secret.

"There," Mrs Walker said, switching off the engine. She turned to smile at the girls. "Do you want me to come in with you?"

Rachel shook her head. "We'll be fine, Mum," she said. "We're meeting Holly near the helter-skelter in ten minutes, so we'll go straight there."

"OK," said Mrs Walker. "I'll be back here at three o'clock to pick you up. Have a good time."

"We will," Kirsty said politely. "Thanks, Mrs Walker. See you later."

The girls went through the park

gates. There was a sign advertising the 'Tippington Variety Show' which was to be held at the end of the week, and Rachel pointed at it. "Mum's got us tickets for that as a treat," she said.

"A variety show…that's one with lots of different kinds of acts on, isn't it?" Kirsty asked.

Rachel nodded. "Yes," she said. "And they're holding auditions for the acts all this week. Today they're auditioning for magicians. Lots of the schools around here have put forward performers, and the best one will get to appear in the Variety Show next Saturday. My friend Holly's been picked from our school to audition, so I said we'd cheer her on…"

Read Madison the Magic Show Fairy to find out what adventures are in store for Kirsty and Rachel!

Enjoy special days with the fairies!

Mia
the Bridesmaid
Fairy

Kate
the Royal Wedding
Fairy

Juliet
the Valentine
Fairy

Trixie
the Halloween
Fairy

Emma
the Easter
Fairy

Belle
the Birthday
Fairy

Also available
as an ebook

Look out for the fabulous Rainbow Magic specials.
Each one features exciting new adventures for
Kirsty, Rachel and a special fairy friend!

www.rainbowmagicbooks.co.uk

Meet the fairies, play games
and get sneak peeks at
the latest books!

www.rainbowmagicbooks.co.uk

There's fairy fun for everyone on
our wonderful website.
You'll find great activities, competitions, stories and
fairy profiles, and also a special newsletter.

Get 30% off all Rainbow Magic books at

www.rainbowmagicbooks.co.uk

Enter the code RAINBOW at the checkout.
Offer ends 31 December 2013.

Offer valid in United Kingdom and Republic of Ireland only.

Win Rainbow Magic Goodies!

There are lots of Rainbow Magic fairies, and we want to know
which one is your favourite! Send us a picture of her and tell
us in thirty words why she is your favourite and why you like
Rainbow Magic books. Each month we will put the entries into
a draw and select one winner to receive a Rainbow Magic
Sparkly T-shirt and Goody Bag!

Send your entry on a postcard to Rainbow Magic Competition,
Orchard Books, 338 Euston Road, London NW1 3BH.
Australian readers should email: childrens.books@hachette.com.au
New Zealand readers should write to Rainbow Magic Competition,
4 Whetu Place, Mairangi Bay, Auckland NZ.
Don't forget to include your name and address.
Only one entry per child.

Good luck!

Meet the Showtime Fairies

Also available as an ebook

Collect them all to find out how Kirsty and Rachel help their magical friends to save the Tippington Variety Show!

www.rainbowmagicbooks.co.uk